A Note from the Author
Michaela Morgan

If you have read *Letter from America* I know you'll enjoy meeting Shelley and Tommo again! If you haven't read it, you can enjoy meeting them for the first time!

This is a story about them and how they were friends. Keeping a good friend can be hard, but having a good friend is great.

When I write a story I make friends with the people in my book. I learn all about them. The more I write about them, the more I find out about them.

I want to write more stories about Tommo and Shelley – so I can find out more about them. Will they be able to stay friends? Will they get closer ...? I can't wait to find out!!

To my buddies

Contents

Chapter 1
London and New York

It was another grey day in London but Tommo felt touched by a sudden little beam of happiness. He had a letter!

There on his tatty old doormat, in his dusty old hallway, lay another letter from America.

A letter for him!

It was a letter from Shelley Devane, that "trendsetter, go-getter and MEGA-MODEST Superstar".

This was Shelley's own description of herself.

She thought you should

BE POSITIVE!!!

Always.

Life for Shelley was full of many colours, CAPITAL LETTERS and plenty of exclamation marks!!!!

Shelley had decorated the back of the envelope. She always did this. In red and yellow, green and blue, purple and orange and pink, with many swirls and loops, it said –

DON'T WORRY!
BE HAPPY!

Tommo had to smile as he picked the letter up from the mat. Shelley could always cheer him up. And he had never needed cheering up as much as he did now.

His life had never been easy.

But now it was a total disaster zone.

He put the letter in his bag to read on the way to school.

* * *

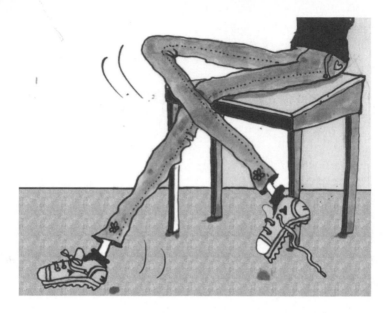

Later that day, in a New York High School, Shelley Devane sat on the edge of her best friend's desk and swung her long, long legs to and fro.

Jade grabbed her bag and pile of books and moved them out of range of Shelley's extra-long legs.

"So, Shelley!" Jade said. "What's new?"

"Tommo should have got my letter today," Shelley smiled. "I should get one back soon."

Jade sighed. "Oh, get real! This letter writing English project stuff is so last year. I stopped writing to my pen pal months ago. Why are you *still* writing to that guy?"

Shelley shrugged. "Well, we're friends now. Real friends. We're not just pen pals now. We're buddies."

Chapter 2
Mail

In London, Tommo was stuck on a crowded bus as it inched its way through the morning rush hour.

Past the SLOW MEN AT WORK sign it went.

Then round the roundabout, and past the line of new shops with their signs –

Tommo was not really looking. He was
waiting for the chance to read his letter. As
soon as he got a seat on the bus he took the
letter out of his bag, ripped it open and
read –

Hey Tommo!

How are you? I LOVED that card you sent. I showed it to Jade and tried to tell her (again) what good friends we've become but she just doesn't get it. This is how it goes when I talk to her:

Jade: How can you be friends with a boy you've never met? A boy you might never meet!

Me: We *might* meet.
I *might* go over to England.
He *might* come over here.

Jade: Pigs *might* fly! I *might* become President of the USA. A duck *might* win the lottery. I *might* get a pet alligator ...

Me: Look, I wrote to Tommo all last year when his family was falling apart. I know what that's like. I helped him over it. We're buddies. You've gotta stick by your buddies.

I've run through all this with her time after time but she doesn't get it at all. I think she's worried that if I'm *your* friend, then *she* won't be my best friend. I've tried and tried to tell her that this is NOT how it is but she just rolls her eyes, sighs and says, "Yeah, yeah. Whatever …"

BUT she has had one good idea (and – no – it's not the one about getting a pet alligator). She said, "Why don't you two just e-mail each other? That school letter writing project is so over now. No one writes LETTERS! Get real!"

I think it's a good idea. What about it?

Write soon – or better yet e-mail shelleydevane@crazyco.com

Your friend,

Shelley (let's move into the 21st century) Devane

Tommo ripped a page out of his rough book and started to write back.

Dear **Shelley,**

Your friend Jade's, "Let's e-mail idea" is great. Just a few tiny problems with it.

The problems are:

1. I don't have an e-mail connection on my computer.

2. In fact, I don't have a computer.

3. They won't let us use school computers to send e-mails to friends.

So it looks as if we're stuck with snail mail.

– at least until your duck wins the lottery and lends me some cash.

Anyway I like keeping your old letters. I keep them in a shoe box in my room and I re-read them sometimes. When I feel down I read some of the things you told me last year and – hey – your advice still works!

It still makes me feel better (or more POSITIVE, as you would say).

It's not easy carrying on after your mum has moved out. It still seems like a dream. And not a good one.

Picture it. It goes like this –

1. You come home from school as normal.

2. You open the door as normal.

3. Then you see an empty hall –

No baby buggy for my little sisters.

No coats and boots.

No toys.

4. You go into the living room –

No table.

No telly.

No computer.

No sofa.

That's what it was like when my mum walked out. She'd gone. She'd taken my two little sisters. She'd taken everything that was useful or nice in the house. She'd even taken the cat but she hadn't taken me.

Sorry – but there's nothing much POSITIVE about that.

I don't talk about it much. My dad just said, "She's gone. And good riddance."

I found out later that she'd rented a small flat – one room really – where she and my baby sisters can just about fit. It's miles away. No room for me.

So I'm left here with Dad in a house full of gaps.

I'm glad I've got you to write to. I don't talk about it at school with my mates. You know how it is. I don't want to be like a hard luck story. My dad *won't* talk about it. So it's good to know you're there.

School's a bit of a pain. My best teacher has left. It was Mrs Sadler. We called her Saddo Sadler but she was all right really. She was the one who started us off on this letter writing project.

Now we've got Mr Sykes. We call him Psycho Sykes – and he really is a psycho.

No idea of a joke.

No idea of fun.

No ideas.

All he has is A VERY LOUD VOICE – and bad breath.

And all he says with this very loud voice is,

"We've had quite enough of your messing about, Thomas Tomlinson. DETENTION!"

I've had so many detentions it's like I'm nearly living at that school.

Still it saves me hanging around in a half-empty house.

So what are you up to? Still dreaming about being a Superstar?

Still crazy about dancing?

Still crazy about music?

Still just crazy?

I'll send you a more cheerful (and POSITIVE) letter next time. Promise.

Hey, and what about YOUR promise to me? You said you would send me a photo. Weeks have passed. Months have passed. Still no photo. Do you look like this?

What are you keeping secret?! Are you trying to be a famous Woman of Mystery?

Write soon,

Tommo 'waiting-for-a-photo' Tomlinson

The bus pulled up outside Tommo's school. Tommo sighed, got off the bus and went into school. Another day.

Chapter 3
Trouble

It was nearly two weeks before Tommo got a reply from Shelley. In those two weeks he had three detentions. All from Psycho.

Tommo didn't feel he could explain about his mum walking out.

So when Psycho bellowed, "Where's your homework diary? Why haven't you got your report card signed? Why is your uniform in

that state?" Tommo just shrugged and
looked at his feet.

"You need to change your attitude," is
what Mr Sykes kept saying.

Mad Attitude

Sad Attitude

Bad Attitude

Glad Attitude
(anyone got one of
these, please?)

In the mornings Tommo had to *make* himself go out the door and set off for school.

Some days he had to make himself get out of bed.

What he really wanted to do was stay in bed all day with his head under the pillow.

In the old days (was it only a few weeks ago?) his mum would have woken him up. She would have made him some toast. There would have been a clean shirt for him.

Not any more.

If he wanted something now, he had to do it himself.

His shirt was hardly ever clean now.

There wasn't anything for breakfast either.

Anyway – at last a letter! Tommo stuffed it in his bag and ran out to catch his bus.

He got to the bus stop just in time to see the bus as it vanished round the corner. Missed it.

That meant a 20-minute wait for the next one. It also meant he would be very, VERY late for school.

Which meant another detention from Psycho.

Tommo made up his mind fast. Instead of waiting at the bus stop he turned round and went into the park. He wouldn't go to school at all.

He sat down on a park bench and opened Shelley's latest letter.

Hey Buddy!! it started. Shelley was excited about something again.

Hey Buddy!!

Guess what! Well you'll never guess – so I'll tell you.

I'm going to be on TV. In a competition. It's called

Teen Superstar.

I have to go along for a test. I have to sing a song and impress the judges. And if they like me (and hey! What's not to like!) I get to go to a special Stage School where they train me to be a star and I GET TO GO ON TV. Everyone will see me.

How great is that?!

All my life I've wished for three things –

1. To be a star

2. To be a star

and

3. To be a STAR!!

And now I have a chance!

I read all about it on a poster and I'm going along for the test. They call it an 'audition'. I'm gonna blow their socks off. And their shoes. Hey, they'd better hang onto their pants! I am gonna be *so* good. Get ready to be blown away by

Shelley Devane!

But have I got work to do! First of all I need a TOTAL make over.

OK, I confess, I haven't sent you a photo 'cos I'm not all that special looking. I'm not a monster. But I'm no Barbie doll either.

I am a bit TOO tall, to tell you the truth. 'Gangly' is another word for it. I seem to have extra long arms and legs. Let me put it this way, if anyone ever needs anything from a high shelf I'm the girl for the job.

The hair – well it's OK but that's about it. Nothing special – just a light brown, mid-length, normal sort of hair.

Kinda frizzy to tell you the truth.

Then there's the clothes. My mom has *no* idea. Not a jot. Whenever I see something *really* cool that I just know I'd look great in she just makes a sort of clicking sound with her teeth.

This means NO.

And so I'm little Miss Normal – but not so very little. I need a new image if I'm going to be a star.

I've asked Jade to give me a mega make over and then I'll have the audition the next day.

I can play guitar. I can play piano. I can dance. I can sing and I can write songs. *I must get through!*

I've written a song to perform.

Here it is:

You guys just HAVE to give me one tiny
chance.
You have to hear me sing. You have to
watch me dance,

'cos I know I have the makings of a real

super star.

I know I have the talent to go *so* far.

So, listen up, and hear my song

And, hey, if you wanna you can sing

along

Sing hey for Shelley!
Shelley Devane!!

If you don't vote for Shelley you'll be so

ashamed.

It's got a very catchy tune. Jade says it's great. It shows off all my talents. How modest is that?!

I'll write and let you know how it goes and I'll send a photo of the new-look-*cool-look*-me.

Your friend,

Shelley (the Superstar) Devane

PS I was thinking about you in your half-empty house with your dad. It sounds terrible. What do you eat? Have you seen your mom yet? Have you asked her why she didn't take you?

I'm guessing she took the babies because they're so little. They need her. Your older brother, Terry, has left home already. Right?

So that leaves you. She must have thought you'd be better off with your dad 'cos you're a boy and 15 and there'd be no room for you in her new place.

Though she does seem to have found room for the TV. And the computer. And the cat.

Write soon and tell me how you're coping. And wish me luck!!!

* * *

Tommo folded the letter up. Shelley sounded so full of life.

In a way it made him feel bad. *This* letter was *not* cheering him up. There she was with all her plans and ideas and he just felt empty. Yes, that was how he felt – as if someone had unplugged him. All his energy had drained away.

He set off slowly to walk home.

Maybe he'd go back to bed.

Back home, in the empty house, he got his homework book, ripped out a page and made a start on his reply to Shelley.

Dear Shelley Superstar,

OK, I wish you luck. Lots of it. But I hope you remember your old friends when you're rich and famous. Maybe you can come and say hi when you're on your world tour?

I'm at home – just me and the cat. Oh yeah – Mum hadn't taken the cat after all. We found it. It was sitting in a box looking grumpy.

I'm bunking off school. First time I've done it. It feels odd. There's no one here at home to see whether I'm at school or not. I don't think my dad cares all that much anyway.

I think he drinks too much. That's the sort of thing my mum said (or *shouted*) at him. Apart from that he's all right but when he drinks he doesn't care much about anything else.

He doesn't care about paying bills.

He doesn't seem to care about Mum.

Or me.

I've tried to get his attention: "Hey, Dad, there's footy on the telly!"

No answer.

"Dad, it's the final – for the cup!"

Not a twitch. "There's a hippo – it's eating the house!"

No response.

He doesn't notice anything. He doesn't care about anything.

So I don't suppose he'll care whether I go to school or not.

He doesn't care much about shopping or eating either. Mum took a lot of stuff with her but she left the freezer. So we've just been eating stuff out of there. Pizza mostly.

I never thought I'd ever get fed up of pizza. But I am. I've started to look like a pizza. I've got big spotty blobs on my face that look like splodges of tomato.

It's not a good look.

We did try to eat some of the other frozen stuff. 'Pop in the microwave for six minutes' it says on the pack. Sounded OK but Mum had taken the microwave. We ended up with de-frosted, uncooked gunk. Back to the pizzas for me.

I haven't seen my mum yet but I'm going to see her on Saturday. I'm going to give her a right ear-bashing.

About your song – I hope it *does* have a good tune because I'm not so sure about the words. I thought of another version for you.

Here it is:

Watch her dance. Hear her sing.

Shelley Devane does her thing.

Feel free to clap, and sing along,

As Superstar Shelley sings her song.

Sing hey for Shelley,

Shelley Devane.

Talented, tall.

And completely insane.

Only joking! I'm sure it'll be wicked!

Let me know.

Tommo (not-terribly-talented-or-tall) Tomlinson

Tommo wrote Shelley's address on the envelope then slunk off to post it. He hoped no one from school spotted him.

Chapter 4
Lucky Break?

Tommo was lucky the first day he bunked off school.

And the next.

And the next.

And the rest.

No one saw him and his dad never noticed. The school phoned his home and

left messages but Tommo simply pressed DELETE. Sorted!

His empty days gave him more time to write to Shelley. He flooded her with notes, complaints, questions and moans.

She replied in her up-beat way, with jokes, good advice – even recipes such as:

Recipe for Blobby Faced Pizza Boy

Take one banana.

Peel away skin.

Eat.

Repeat with various fruit.

And Zap those Zits!

She gave him up-dates on her 'act' too.
The dances she'd worked on. The songs
she'd written. The high hopes she had.

Tommo stayed away from school. He
bunked off day after day and it looked as if
he was getting away with it.

But his luck couldn't last.

It was Friday morning, and Tommo was
at the Post Office again. He was getting
more stamps for letters to America when he
saw her. Mrs Sadler – his old teacher!

She had her new baby in a buggy and a pile of envelopes in her hand. She turned and smiled at Tommo.

"Thomas!" she said. "How are you doing?"

"All right," Tommo muttered.

"Still writing to America, I see!" She gave him a big smile. "I'm pleased that seems to have worked out for you ..." She stopped and looked at him. "Hang on ... shouldn't you be in school?"

Tommo tried to act cool. He muttered something about dentists but he knew his ears had gone bright red and he knew Mrs Sadler could tell he was lying.

"Post your letter," she said. "Then we'll have a little chat. OK?"

* * *

One hour, one large Coke, fries and burger later and he had blurted it all out. He hadn't meant to. He had tried to stay cool. He had tried to lie but Mrs Sadler knew him too well. She had taught him for two years and she had never been easy to mess with.

She sat him at a table in a burger bar. She took her time. She bought him food, she listened and she looked. She saw the new crumpled looking Tommo. She spotted how quickly he ate. Saw his new slumped look. His grey and red blotched skin. She dragged little bits of information out of him and then guessed the rest.

"Do you know where you are?" she said at last.

"In a burger bar," Tommo shrugged.

She smiled. "You are at a turning point – that's where you are. This is where you choose how the rest of your life goes."

Tommo scowled and slurped the rest of his Coke.

"I'm serious," she said. "This is your growing up moment. This is where you take charge. It's time to decide who you will be."

Tommo was puzzled. "What d'you mean?" he asked.

"The way I see it," she said, "the things you're getting in trouble for at school are all linked to your mum leaving. Am I right?"

"Suppose so …" Tommo admitted.

"And neither you, nor your dad, nor your mum has told the school about what's happened. Right?"

"Well, y ... yes ..." Tommo could guess where this was going.

"Tomorrow," said Mrs Sadler, "you could bunk off school again. Maybe you'll get away with it again. But each time you do, it will be harder to go back. Things will just get worse.

There is another way. You could go in and see your head of year, Mr Robinson. He's OK, you know. You could tell him about everything – just like you've told me. I promise you, it will make things easier. You shouldn't have to pretend everything's OK and hide what's really going on. It's making life too hard for you."

On and on she went.

She didn't give up easily.

"I'll think about it," Tommo agreed in the end. "That's *all* I promise. I'll think about it."

They left it at that.

Chapter 5
Breaking Up

Shelley's next letter began like this –

Oh Tommo – Total
disaster!!!

My life is RUINED!

Tommo had just finished talking to Mr
Robinson. It had been hard. He felt weird.
He held his breath. What disaster had
happened to Shelley?

Had her mum walked out too?

Had her dad turned into a slumped
figure in an armchair?

Had Shelley had to admit all this to a teacher and then hear words like 'Social Services' and 'Care'?

But no.

That wasn't why Shelley was upset.

Her make over had not worked out.

And she had fallen out with Jade.

Tommo sighed. Girls! Sometimes they were just stupid. He read on:

I will never forgive Jade.

She has turned me into a clown.

She said she was going to "tidy" my eyebrows.

Result?

I now look as if I've been plugged into the mains.

She was going to "bring my hair to life with a hint of red".

Result?

I now look like a total carrot.

She said she was giving my hair a trim. "Just spike it up a bit", she said.

Result?

I now look like a hedgehog.

I had to go to the audition with my carrot colour, hedgehog hair and no eyebrows.

The panel of celebrities looked shocked. Who can blame them?

I was a disaster.

A big flop.

So that's the end of my life as a star.

And that's the end of my friendship with so-called best friend Jade.

I'll never speak to her again.

Shelley 'rock-bottom' Devane

The more he read, the more angry Tommo was.

He wasn't angry with Jade but he was FURIOUS with Shelley.

He had just had one of the hardest times of his life. It had taken every scrap of his courage to go into school again. And to ask to see Mr Robinson. And then to tell him about his mum and dad. Somehow having to tell his Head of Year all that had happened made it seem more real. Tommo was worried sick about what would happen next.

And now here was Shelley not thinking about him at all. Instead she was going on and on about her hair cut.

He wrote back right away –

Dear So—called Best Buddy Shelley Devane,

So your hair colour is a bit brighter than normal. What a shame.

It's cut a bit short and your eyebrows are a bit strange. Well, boo hoo. Sorry if I don't care as much as you'd like me to but have you heard yourself? How selfish and small-minded can you be?

First there's Jade, your so-called life-long best friend. She didn't mean the make over to go wrong, did she? She must feel terrible. And now you won't talk to her. What sort of a friend are you to Jade?

And what sort of a friend are you to me?

You just don't know how bad things are for me. I've just been to talk to my Head of Year. I had to tell him that I've been bunking off school. I've had to tell him all about my family – and me. And I don't like talking about personal stuff. I hate it. I felt sick. I nearly threw up. And you say your life's "ruined" – because your hair-style turned out wrong. You don't ask about me at all! Not one question about me. Just thinking about yourself. You're as bad as my mum and dad.

I can't believe it. I thought you were clever and understanding and a true friend.

I was wrong.

You're no friend of mine.

Goodbye. I don't want to hear from you ever again.

Tommo

Tommo stuffed the letter into the envelope and posted it quickly. *That's the end of my friendship with so-called best buddy Shelley Devane!* he thought. *She's gone – and good riddance!*

Chapter 6
Buddies?

After that there was a long silence.

No letters.

Days went by.

Weeks went by.

Tommo's doormat stayed empty. And after all his anger, Tommo felt empty too. He felt bad. He missed those sunbeam moments when he saw a letter on the doormat waiting for him. He felt lost.

"So what?" he told himself. "Why should I care? She's gone and good riddance!" That's just what his dad had said when his mum had gone. Then his dad had fallen apart and given up.

"Looks like I'm just as much of a saddo as he is." Tommo smiled a bitter smile.

* * *

Then one Saturday afternoon

Dringggg!

The phone rang.

RRRRRRING!
Rrrrrring!

Tommo answered it.

"Is that Tommo?" said a voice.

His heart missed a beat. It was a girl's voice. An American girl's voice.

"I ... I is that Shelley?" he stammered.

"No, dork brain, it isn't. It's Jade. D'you know who I am?"

"Yeah ..." Tommo began. "How did you get my number?"

"International Directories, lame brain. Now, listen up. I haven't got long. If my mom finds I'm making a call to London she'll flip. But you have to know what you've done.

I've never seen Shelley like this. She's so totally down and depressed.

First I make her look like a clown. The other kids really gave her a hard time.

Then she fails that audition. Boy! Were they nasty to her – on national TV too. They keep replaying it on the opening credits. Three times now, I've seen it. The 'panel' of judges being oh so clever and oh so witty and oh so cruel and Shelley trying to smile and look bright when any fool can see she's trying not to cry on TV.

Then, just when she needs a friend most, she gets that letter from you. Well, I'm here to tell you, buddy, no one – NO ONE – messes with my best friend like that!"

"I thought you weren't friends any more." Tommo managed to get a word in.

"Oh that!" she said. "We got over that! That's what REAL friends do. They make up. You should try it sometime. It's not rocket science."

"But ..." Tommo got no further.

"Yikes – my mom's coming. Oh ..."

Beeeeep!

*   *   *

Long after the call had finished, Tommo held on to the phone. His mind was racing. So was his heart.

Had his letter really hurt Shelley so much?

Did she care so much about what he thought of her?

Could he be the one to help her – instead of her being the one to help him?

Had he really been selfish?

But hadn't *she* been selfish?

Had they *both* been selfish?

His mind was in a whirl but one thing he knew – he wanted to contact Shelley again.

*   *   *

He went to get paper and a pen, then he sighed. It was so slow.

S   L   O   W.

It would be days and days before she got his letter. He wanted to speak to her NOW. He looked at the phone.

What if he called International Directories and asked for Shelley's number – like Jade had done? How did you get International Directories? What would he say? Then his mind was made up for him. He heard his dad moving around upstairs. If his dad found him phoning America there would be real trouble!

He checked the credit on his mobile. No way! Maybe he should try a phone box then? He put his hands in his pockets. £3.40. Was that enough money to phone America? He didn't think so.

Maybe he could try to e-mail from school. But that wasn't allowed. Then the answer came to him – the Internet café he'd seen from the bus. *That's it*, he thought. He checked his money again. He did have enough. He'd go there now.

Fifteen minutes later he was sitting in the Internet café.

And he had already keyed in shelleydevane@crazyco.com

He stared at the blank screen. What could he say? How do you start? Jade had said it was easy to make up. "That's what real friends do," she had said. "It's not rocket science."

It felt like rocket science to him.

He took a deep breath and started

Dear Shelley,

I'm sorry ...

Barrington Stoke would like to thank all its readers for commenting on the manuscript before publication and in particular:

Sonya Akhtar
Shahzabe Ali
Cheryl Anderson
Mrs Blake
Cherie Borthwick
Thomas Brogan
Aimi Burrows
Charlotte Butler
Callum Chambers
Jessie Clark
Declan Deeny
Sunaina Deol
David Dinwoodie
Louise Docherty
Brogan Donachie
Mrs Duffell
Mrs Duffy
Amy Evans
Erin Gillies
Kirsty-Louise Hunt
Lauren Kennedy

Zoe King
Vhari Kingsman
Mark Mabon
Kris Maltman
Megan Morcombe
Marc O'Donnell
Melissa Pacey
Jill Pattison
Guy Robertshaw
Ann Robson
Gursimaran Roth
Daryll Scott
Ashley Settle
Guy Shaw
Megan Simms
Mrs Bridget Smith
Craig Smith
Susan Stewart
Frances Underhill
Carol Williams

Become a Consultant!

Would you like to give us feedback on our titles before they are published? Contact us at the e-mail address below – we'd love to hear from you!

info@barringtonstoke.co.uk
www.barringtonstoke.co.uk

Have you read the first Tommo and Shelley story?

Letter from America
by Michaela Morgan

Tommo's fed up. His teacher has had another of her ideas. She wants everyone in the class to have a pen pal. Tommo knows it's going to be boring, boring, BORING. But he's in for a big surprise! Share Tommo's sad times and his happy times – and meet Shelley who raps, rhymes and jokes in her letters from America.

You can order *Letter from America* directly from our website at www.barringtonstoke.co.uk

Also by the same author ...

PomPom
by Michaela Morgan

Have you ever wished you had a dog? Paul dreams of having a champion dog to improve his image. But when he is forced to look after PomPom, a soppy, fluffy, girly *poodle*, he nearly dies of embarrassment. But maybe this dog is cooler than it looks ...

You can order *PomPom* directly from our website at www.barringtonstoke.co.uk